+ + +

"A collection of modern myths or extended prose poems, *boysgirls* asks questions about the minutiae of enchantment and its attendant quotidian... [Farris] has constructed a chimerical work, more poetry than prose, a disordered mythology, a book of secrets almost told...and invents new myths from old... the palimpsest, the always erased, as the only thing that endures... Katie Farris will lead you. It will never be to where you think you are going or want to go, but you will need to go there, even to the precipice."

—ROBERT LIPTON, *Poetry Flash*

+ + +

"Farris insolently promises to provide fiction that you will be forced to react to, something unique, something you will want to keep reading—and then she insolently makes good on that promise."

—DEBRAH LECHNER, *Hayden's Ferry Review*

+ + +

"*boysgirls* is an extraordinary book. Without exaggeration, reading it, I felt as if the top of my head was taken off, to use Emily Dickinson's words. I love the experience and intensity of this language on the page, the dark magic fairy-tale world of it. I love how Farris can forge an eloquent lyricism out of a language that is stronger than cast iron. It is incredible."

—Malena Mörling, Guggenheim Fellow & author of *Ocean Avenue*

boysgirls

boysgirls

katie farris

T P

boysgirls
Copyright © 2011 Katie Farris. All rights reserved.

Introduction and Afterword Copyright © 2019 Tupelo Press.
All rights reserved.

Library of Congress Catalog-in-Publication data available
upon request.
ISBN paperback: ISBN-13: 978-1-946482-27-3

Illustrations by Lavinia Hanachiuc
Design: Allison Carr (2011 edition), Kenji Liu (2019 edition)

2nd edition: September 2019

Tupelo Press
P.O. Box 1767
North Adams, Massachusetts 01247
(413) 664-9611 / Fax: (413) 664-9711
editor@tupelopress.org / www.tupelopress.org

Tupelo Press is an award-winning independent literary
press that publishes fine fiction, non-fiction, and poetry in
books that are a joy to hold as well as read. Tupelo Press is
a registered 501(c)(3) non-profit organization, and we rely
on public support to carry out our mission of publishing
extraordinary work that may be outside the realm of the large
commercial publishers. Financial donations are welcome and
are tax deductible.

contents

a preface to katie farris' *boysgirls*

KRISTINA MARIE DARLING

In her recent study, *The End of Gender: A Psychological Autopsy*, Shari L. Thurer asserts that "Clearly, much of what we call sexual orientation and gender identity is socially constructed. Yet for all of its fluidity, it remains unruly, impervious to will." In other words, our understanding of sexuality embodies, at its very core, a contradiction. The enactment of gender identity is pure artifice and invention, and, at the same time, an otherness that speaks through the subject. For Thurer, this performance of gender is not self-expression, as we tend to define it, but rather, it is a narrative over which we often lack agency, awareness, and control.

Katie Farris' *boysgirls* fully does justice to the complexities inherent in our understanding of gender. Presented in an impressive array of hybrid forms, ranging from flash fiction to prose poetry, the texts contained in this theoretically astute volume embrace contradictions and liminal places. As the book unfolds, these bright apertures come to encompass the space between genres and discourses, as well as provocative and unfamiliar ways of performing gender identity.

Farris warns us, *"These are not stories one can hand to another and afterward ask: did your soul move like the peristalsis inside your gut?"* Instead of capitalizing on the satisfying and familiar conventions of narrative, she uses the unclassifiable text, the monstrous text, and unruly prose to explore the ways language, as we know it, limits what is possible in our thinking about gender. For Farris, genre—with its established conventions, its repertoire of restrictions – and gender are inexorably linked. Indeed, she shows us that our most familiar categories of identity are embedded within the very texture of language itself. She reveals form, genre, and even grammar as the foundation of the social order, that alterity which speaks through us and, at the same time, defines us.

For Farris, new ways of being in the world require new forms of discourse, as they call for a vehicle that fully does justice to their nuances. She states, for example, in a recent interview in *The Kenyon Review*, "Hybrid-form works stand on thresholds, refusing definition and creating themselves out of necessity. When I say that they are created from necessity, I mean that I think these works are best suited to communicate ideas that have never been communicated before: a new form *must* be created to contain them. The impossible becomes possible with hybrid forms." Throughout *boysgirls*, these liminal spaces afford an opportunity for transcendence. As the poet Myung Mi Kim once argued, the apertures are places where the rules of discourse no longer hold.

Fittingly, Farris' transformations are revolutions in poetic language as much as they challenge familiar narratives that circulate within culture. As she herself writes, "*the story has been changed. It is my body. Eat from it and live.*"

O o o o o Madness! To you I sing—to you
I dedicate—I sing my praises to you.

Article **5**

There are ways of telling a story, they say, so that it comes alive. In the quaint way of stories. Meaning we may be mesmerized. Meaning we may begin to sketch out, in the eyes of our mind, a more or less spectacular vision. What this does not mean is that my hand, my madwoman's hand, neatly manicured with a certain fragile glowing in my too-white skin, will reach out to take you, dear reader, by the throat. I can feel you swallowing. It's a natural reflex to having your esophagus squeezed. Each of the cartilaginous rings that prop your windpipe open trembles under my touch, your Adam's apple, the slightly *greasy place where you dabbed your perfume. What is it you hope to accomplish by reading this book? You were hoping to escape unscathed?*

You're used to sitting back and eavesdropping, playing the voyeur on the lives of others. But between these covers you will participate, whether you desire it or not. You might think about this before you turn the page. You might turn the page.

This is the new literature.

In this world (of which I am the author) I am not the only denizen, citizen, harlequin, or doyenne. I have invented myself, surely, who hasn't, but I, unlike (perhaps) you, have also invented others—assorted godlettes, hopefuls, poseurs, and freaks. Still, we're closer than you might think, reader. In fact, if you take this opportunity to examine yourself in the mirror, is that not me, there, in the shadow of your nostril, or setting free those pesky strands of hair around your part? Don't be afraid! I know my place. Let me entertain you! I'm only here to make you smile, never to think, never to think.

Underneath your skin, you might look something like this: bibles make up your brow, and your nose is a chunk of bacon. Your lips lie like two dolphins tight against your jaw, which is a golden cage where your teeth, like soldiers, line up to the march of your heart. But your eyes, they are glorious. They lie, curled up in their soft round beds, rolling and turning like newborn mice below the blankets of your eyelids. Beautiful. You are beautiful.

Do not fear, dear reader. We will not attempt to throw you down from your throne. We are all aware (shh! shh!) that we are here to please. Enjoy our ghastly pirouettes, then, our silhouettes, afterwards our plucky monologues et cetera. We are here for the purpose of being beautiful. Please do not attempt to use us otherwise.

Who is to say anyway that hallucinations are things to be avoided? On the contrary, raise your cup to a new standard! Toss aside the past and drink deeply of this deep. Never fear, there are no Romantic fools here, just bread and circus bread and circus bread and circus.

It is time to laugh, to free that deep itch in your tongue,

it is time to show your violet-tinged teeth and guffaw despite
that twitch in your disapproving lover's buttocks, the spasm
in your mother's lower spine. Come giddy yourself atop these
sheer drops. Come shake victorious with delirium tremens
and carpe diem. Come frolic with bared teeth.

girls

mise en abyme

People are forever falling for the girl with a mirror for a face. And why not? they think, not unaware of the irony. Of course, one has to be careful in direct sunlight. But just imagine: if stranded on a desert island, who could resist the siren song of the girl with a mirror for a face? Rescue would come posthaste!

One morning a passerby notices her sitting high over the city in the morning light. Her face is a map more beautiful than the most exalted cartographer's. In her face, it's so clear that the city provides, provides, provides. Its spires plunge upward. The bald appear follicular, the paunchy slender. The city commissions a portrait of the girl with a mirror for a face, then orders all past images of itself destroyed. After viewing the portrait, even the most skinflint of council members vote to begin building a metro based on the veinwork of the human body. A policy like that can make inroads surprisingly quickly.

The girl is glad that people love her, happy to have something to reflect, for she had felt most intimately anguished, attenuated as she was to the nuances of nothingness. For have you ever looked into a mirror with another mirror? Nothing reflected back into nothing. An infinity of nothing.

Still, given her druthers, the girl with a mirror for a face would give up all her notoriety and wish first for a mouth. She reflects on all the mouths made for devouring: bee-mouth, moth-mouth, the various mouths of months, babybird beaks, the liquidating straw-mouth of the seastar, the lamprey's edgy round electric hole. But it is men

she finds most beautiful. To watch men eating
something difficult, something with bones, is
to watch an animal testing himself against chips,
cracks, and breakage. Some eat for power, some
for beauty. Sometimes food is not food at all, but
stones, or words, or angry bees disguised in honey.
The girl with a mirror for a face would like her
own mouth, so as to be less empty. The girl with a
mirror for a face would like to be full of homely
peanuts, pitted olives, octopus ink, and fillets of
thin white-boned fish.

On days when she feels hungry, when there
is no one around to reflect, she takes comfort in
this fact: the number zero was invented to act as a
placeholder in calculations, indicating the degree
of loss or gain. And so I am not only empty, the girl
thinks—I also contain multitudes.

the girl who grew

I know what I look like, lying in this muddy water, my toes and fingers thick as the trunks of elephants, my eyes rusted almost shut with pondweed and petrified eyelashes. A giant doll of a woman, though my eyes no longer open and close. But. You came to hear a fairy tale? Hear:

✦✦✦

When anyone asked the girl what she wanted

for Christmas, she told them history books
or crystals for her collection. But the desire
that lit her darkest nights was to grow up.

One summer night, she did grow. As she slept,
she grew extraordinarily tall; she wound herself
tighter and tighter into her bed to fit. When she
woke, her head kissed the ceiling. All that day she
watched in wonder as people ran from her, and
she was satisfied. She let go a laugh that haunted
children into the arms of their mothers, and
the mothers into the arms of their fathers, and
fathers into the arms of the churches. Still, she
kept growing.

That first day she drank forty-seven pails of
milk drawn from the sides of gentle cows; she
gorged on blackberry brambles and their thorns
and stingers tickled down her throat. She ate the
cats and dogs of her torturers and was gratified by
their tiny cries. Soon she was as tall as buildings, as
trees. At the end of that day her mania ended, and
she was sorry for eating the cats and dogs (although

not for anything else), and she helped the town rebuild by lifting logs and other rubble daintily between her first finger and thumb.

She lived in a nearby bog, where she ate only vegetation and the tiny eggs of birds, for she had lost her taste for meat. She found she liked to sleep standing up, liked waking for those lost quiet minutes in the middle of the night and looking down on the town through her half-closed eyes. Knowing she cast a shadow. She lived like this for many years, one day tearing down the waterwheel, overturning silos and greedily eating the ripened barley, the next sowing entire fields with one cast of her arm, or harvesting rows and rows of corn in a few sun-laden minutes, one stalk hanging lazily between her teeth like a shaft of wheat.

The people of the town, in turn, made offerings to the girl who grew: wheels of cheeses, vats of cream, salads of enormous seaweed flats brought in from the shore, a day's truck-ride away. The town became known for breeding enormous poultry that laid eggs bigger than a man's head—for her, the size of a delicate currant. After many years, she was twenty stories tall, but no taller, and nine years old, but no older.

And she was feared, and needed, and powerful.

+ + +

And here the fairy tale ends. I was powerful, needed, yes, but fear... fear is what completes this story.

There was a drought. People suffered and could not stop suffering. It was not the middle ages, little man, but it might as well have been. A witch-hunt, with no witch, and no hunt. They knew right where to find me.

I was sleeping, standing as was my habit. The crowd could have been mice for all the attention I paid. The first blow of the axe tickled my ankle, but didn't wake me. Then it stung, and I scratched it with the toe of my other shoe, killing a man (my first, my only, my accident). Next, a chainsaw on a brave ladder hamstrung me. Crashing to the ground, to my knees, I was awake and blinded with pain and I cried so loud everyone's eardrums shattered and blood leaked from their ears and then we were all, all of us, in pain.

When I woke up things were much as they are now. Here is the rock that was my foot, and here the rock that was my shoulder. Do you see what I am turning into? The ocean could be my bath, the clouds a corona round my head. This is what I know: that regimes of fear end in pain. Patent leather holds up remarkably well in swamp water. That people forget. That it is no pain to be forgotten.

the politics
of metamorphosis

Although generally you will not find it to be so, in this village the girl's belly is held in high esteem. Her husband, dead after his tractor ran over an unseen rock and capsized, left his seed there. They crowded her to protect her from the sight of his death, for she was almost ready to give birth. The child! The child! they whisper, pressing against her with their somber, sweaty hands (for her husband was a loved man, a powerful man). They crowd her in the hopes that she will birth something better than they are.

Suddenly she is a part of—what? In stories, girls
are changed into cows or trees or rivers, or they are
made to lie with swans and bulls and rivers. Even
eating an innocent berry on the forsaken moor can
get one pregnant by some vegetable god.

They say that the girl has ripened, is about to
produce fruit. Her husband would not have fruited,
ripened, even if he hadn't died. And so the girl has
learned that the location of her metamorphosis is
her womb. But what does the girl want? And what
about the womb?

The girl cannot breathe. The child moves like
an earthquake within her, shows its handprint,
its footprint, through the skin of her belly. The
girl wants it to wrap its hand around her finger.
She wants it out. She wants be alone. She wants
nothing more than to steal chocolates and crouch
someplace alone, hidden, alone, to eat.

The girl runs. She runs until she feels a warning
spasm in her back. She stops at the graveyard. She
can see that the last season of digging found the

same old dirt buried beneath the new ashes, the new bones, beneath the midden heap and the broken crockery, beneath the stories that couldn't change, beneath the this and the that of the words the villagers speak. It is clear, she reminds herself, that a bone is a bone, no matter where it's found.

her mother's mother was a machete

Her mother's mother was a machete. For her sixth birthday the girl received her mama's pelt, laid down like the skin of a selkie, and a room in her grandmother's house.

Every morning, the girl picked her grandmother up by her red splintered handle, cradling her silver head in the crook of her arm, and carried her to the kitchen table, where she sat and smoked with gale force while downing cups of coffee. The girl didn't know where the smoke went, but she spent her days mopping the floor from stove to refrigerator. They listened to Christian talk radio. They supported themselves making dolls from straw: the girl split the strands against her grandmother's well-honed blade.

Sometimes the grandmother let the girl sandpaper her handle, or re-glue her haft. On such occasions she made the girl turn her in front of the mirror, murmuring, "Aren't you delightful. I used to be a beautiful blade. Look at me now. I used to be beautiful." After they watch the moon rise, the girl carries her grandmother back to her bedroom, lowers the blinds, pulls the covers up around her shoulder's blade. Heads back to her own room. Opens her Bible to Ezekiel. To Job. Ruth. More of that strange mourning. But the grandmother doesn't die, and doesn't die, and doesn't die, until she does.

cyclops

The maker kept making her, long after she was finished. The girl had an overcooked quality, singed brittle round the edges. Separate things—toes and fingers, eyes, lips—had run all together. Stumps for arms. Stumps for feet. Mute for mouth. Cyclops. She looks like a lumberer, but her passages are soft, as is her eye, colorful as a whorled marble.

The scientists come from everywhere to make a study of the girl. She pirouettes in hospital gowns, is the gracious acceptor of injections and prodding fingers, trembles charmingly before their photographic lenses. She loves to hear them say her name, loves the circular sound of cyclops, psyclops eyeclops, like a horse galloping over their tongues.

The girl holds out both dry palms, so, and between them there is air, and this is the shape of loss. The girl lectures the scientists on the Manners of Loss, the Occasions of Loss, the Style of Loss, even, with appropriate palettes and tailoring. Her lectures have been published in the House of Infinite Loss in the unmappable Infinite City. (Picture, if you will, the sideways-slanted 8 that signifies that which has no beginning and no end. For loss has no beginning and no end.)

Scientists are interested in Loss as a subject matter, but much more interested in the girl. She has so many seams—between toe and toe, finger and finger, the place where her earflap would have met her head. Her head so smooth and hairless— no strangely shaped cartilage, no Roman bridge or fleshly earlobe. Just that eye, blue and green and brown, roaming moist within its socket. No

pupil, no white sclera: all iris, all rainbow. The girl
lived on only one thing, that thing that must not
be named.

*We near the end now; perhaps she can break the spell.
She leans over, paints it on the back of your hand. Your
mouth curves in a derisive smile. Of course. But you watch
her fade away and feel suddenly old, tired of this irony, your
only companion. It has come and gone. Let it.*

Now begin.

the devil's face

The girl has been learning how to shit on the devil's face. It is a slow process. First of all, one has to take into consideration the setting. In order for the devil to get a hard-on, he must be surrounded at eight points.

To the north, above the devil's head, a soul writhing in eternal agony. On his right hand, a man with infinite bowels being disemboweled, infinitely. At his feet, a vain woman looks into a mirror where boils rise continuously to the surface of her face. To his left, a quiet old man masturbates. To the northeast and southeast, solemn demons.

Northwest and southwest, fallen angels snivel. It is difficult, he explains, after millennia of existence, to get off.

The girl finds it hard to move her bowels properly under the circumstances. She is constipated, seized up, she anticipates the look of disgust on the face of the masturbating man; the angels in their chains rattle in a most distracting manner, and the castor oil has not yet kicked in. She bears down, she changes her position to a squat, she balances herself on the shoulders of one angel and one demon. The devil looks at her with the familiar look of a man about to come, who needs just one more, just one more thing.

The girl has been taking 25 mg of hydroxyzine, an anti-anxiety medication, to deal with her difficulties shitting on the devil's face. She feels it a personal failure; she has never failed to fulfill a man sexually. She doesn't think to blame it on the fact that he has never been a man.

She blames herself but also the fetish and

moreover the look on the devil's face, possessive
and mocking under his thin beard, as if daring
her anus to discharge. The next time the situation
is arranged, the dais well-lit, the tortured man
mocking her with his ropes and ropes of loosened
bowel, she mounts the devil, then turns to face his
horny corny feet. He grunts, he is displeased. She
turns to leer at the masturbating man; noticing for
the first time how lopsided he is—how massive
his right arm, how puny his left! He turns away,
ashamed by her frank stare.

And it is this, this mutual shame, this turning
away, that finally moves her.

how to tame a lion

No coy Leo, he. Who comes toward the girl on great crushing paws, each deadly scythe sheathed in membrane and muscle. He stinks of blood and bison and clean cat sweat. The girl knows she mustn't look him in the eye.

He circles and she scarcely breathes, though her breath is quickening, though her feet are preparing to quicken, and wouldn't it be glorious to run through the mazy cobblestoned alleys with this great tawny feline in powerful pursuit, her threatened blood throbbing thrillingly in her veins, his nose wide abrupt and square in his untamed face? The girl is no lamb either, with a rifle in her hand and the eye to use it.

Instead he stretches, opening his mouth, clean as a cat, and licks her from top to bottom. Nipped in the nape (thankfully draped with her thick hair), she feels the gloss of teeth on the back of her neck. Where his fur is thin he is pink as a man.

(*And what to do with them now, in this semi-truce, this brief glorious interlude between the chase and what is to come? Her adrenaline has come and gone, his paws are heavy on her shoulders and his rich damp breath against her neck begins to sickify her, make her dizzy, nauseated. And yet there is something metamorphic about this moment, no? Like a god, then, we decide: let them be, close the door, turn out the lights. For once, just for once, goddamnit, leave them to their privacy.*)

the hierarchy
of freaks

It is a bad day and age for the kind of freaks we used to be: tattooed ladies, fat women, rubber-faced babas, those mermaid girls with sweet webbed feet. Melancholy freaks, wistful in our gauzy dresses or our striped unitards, every hair in place, with a ready song or a line of verse. Before every man was a mark, there was an etiquette.

Now they want more! Better! Gills! Pinheads! Hermaphrodites! There are specialists of all sorts, with no skills to speak of. Just simple insults to the eyeballs. We used to want to educate our freaks, have them perform moonlight sonatas, play games with the children, woo our women with their tender hearts. Now they watch us on the television, isolated in our own wards, providing no entertainment except in our very formities.

And the state of the freak show? No one takes pride of place in the bally, all the good mikemen have gone the way of the buffalo. It's irony that's ruined this country, the people in it. You treat your freaks as if you've seen it all before.

I don't take these things lightly, you know—if a tear happens to spring from my ductless eyes, what of it? What care you wandering by the fleabitten stadium with our threadbare plush? After you've knocked a good tip into some carnie's pocket for your girl? After you've slummed in the sugar shack and taken a ride on the Ferris wheel to cop that first feel. It's heavier than you expected, isn't it?

I remember it as if it were yesterday, my first day on the box. "Worm Girl" was emblazoned everywhere in royal purple and gold, arrows all

over the show pointing down to me and they came
to me with wonder in their eyes and they touched
me, the places where arm or leg would have been.
Wriggling for them was the necessary evil. But
the looks on their faces when I sang an aria from
Carmen, or the national anthem (I knew several: I
had travelled the globe), the way their eyes filled—
it was as if they didn't even know what they had
come looking for.

a riddle

Tiresias didn't know the half of it. Actually, he only knew halves. Aristophanes spoke of my kind but with two faces. I am the whole. You are a paltry part.

Still, it is lonely. It isn't supposed to be. Alpha and Omega I am.

What am I?

boys

the boy with
one wing

He stands on a beach and tries to resist the wind in his feathers. Painful now, wrenching, the wind on the wing. Twisting wing away from body. Rising wing above the body, the body heavy now, no longer light with hollowed bones and flight. A halfway boy. The Boy stands at the water knowing he's no longer a boy, knowing; he hasn't been a boy for a long time. Knowing he will always be a boy.

The Boy looks around. The Boy thinks he is alone. He tries a few half-hearted, embarrassed leaps off the smaller boulders on the beach, hoping to glide for at least a moment before he lands back on the earth, but he just jars his knees with the weight of his landing.

Still, the women in the town are compelled by him: the rise of his shoulder and cheekbones, his half-winged awkwardness. Imagining only the stroke of feather across skin, her arching back, not the difficulty of cleaning a wing without a beak.

Swans mate for life, don't they? whispers the cheerleader later, the roundness of top and bottom bursting like proud and ruffled feathers from her uniform, pressing up against him quick in a hallway pressing her words to his ear, setting him to burning as she plucks one molting feather and leaves as quickly as he comes.

Times are hard for dreamers, people whisper, watching him. He would like to turn back. Not a dreamer, he would tell them. The dream.

the inventor of
invented things

He is an inventor of invented things—light, for instance, the printing press, three different types of scopes (micro-, tele-, and laryngo-). He invented collard greens and beet greens and dandelion greens, olive oil and sea salt and finely aged vinegars decanted into elaborate systems of spouted and handled glassware; he invented soft sides of risotto, sweet forest mushrooms, knew how to change chemistry into biology, though he soon forgot. Not to be confused with a scientist (when the Inventor of Invented

Things looks in a mirror, all he sees is silvered glass),
he scratches himself with springs as he puzzles over
diagrams. Astounded by pipes, the fulfillment of
their curve, a cylinder within a cylinder, he works
for years on a prototype that will never be realized.

Over the course of twenty, thirty, forty
years he averaged four, then ten, then twelve
inventions a year. He invents things out of order,
for practicality's sake: the ballpoint before the
quill. Then again, his planning hasn't always been
strategic—sexual intercourse came too late in his
life for children, and floss too late for his teeth. He
cannot distinguish the value of things: internal
combustion motors, wheel spokes, the violoncello.
He invented his own life, they say. Never growing
old. People ask. He answers. He has never figured
out how to make bread. He may die trying.

a brief interlude
for seduction

One night, a woman stalks the Boy with One Wing with the confidence we freaks feel before other freaks. She runs, stumbling on cracked sidewalks, smelling the approaching rain and lilacs of early summer. Frightened of her heavy breathing and the sounds of her shoes slipping on the damp grass, the Boy with One Wing hides behind a gravestone, holds his breath, says an apologetic prayer to the dead.

She slides in a mud-track laid down by some landscaper's truck, ends up on her back where she laughs, makes as if to get up, then falls back with a sigh. She counts stars. She feels the seep of cool water. He watches her breasts rise and fall and feels a stir. The Boy with One Wing has lived too long in the imaginations of others.

He stumbles out from behind the gravestone, looks down on her. She looks up. They are very still. Above them, somewhere, a meteor shower. Bright streaks of light. He goes down to his knees and sloshes over to her, one knee before the other, holding his wing up out of the mud. She watches the feathers tremble in the breeze, settles herself more firmly into the earth. Both minds seem as undisturbed by thought as they are by the inevitability of this action, as he lowers himself, propped on one arm, over her. Lips meet, the usual struggle ensues. When he rolls away they look up at the sky. Still, no words are said, and the Boy with One Wing begins to wonder if he's forgotten how to speak.

doldrums

The Boy with One Wing stands freely swinging his arm in the doldrums of this utter night, his joy a burning thing. He's heard of a man who makes flying machines a man who has flown. The Boy with One Wing has known love, and he has known flight. He would give one up for the other. He has made his appointment.

the invention of love

The Boy with One Wing sits in a waiting room, watching people enter, leave, examine the waitlist, attempt appointments. They carry their most precious, destroyed things. The medicine that worked, that no longer works. A beloved, putrefying pet. Many marriages sit broken, waiting for repair by the Inventor of Invented Things. He invented penicillin and Prozac, and is said to have an open mind about inventing poultices, places, and prostheses. Marriage was in fact the Inventor's first invention, but he does not consider himself a counselor, a pet cemeterian, a revivalist, or a pharmacologist. Occasionally he has his secretary drive everyone out of the waiting room, but they all come back, waiting for sometimes weeks, eating only what's in the vending machine.

The Boy with One Wing has been here for a month. Can barely lift his head to look when he hears that inner door open. He is weak from dehydration, from living off sips from the water cooler, but when the Inventor sees him for the first time—gaunt, molting, humped in his seat toward the heavy wing—he can only will his flaccid diaphragm to move.

The Inventor of Invented Things opens his eyes, finds himself cradled in the Boy's one wing. He does not consider the implications of his momentary unconsciousness, does not ask the gravitational consequences of his weight on the boy's hollow bones, does not question the curious melanation of the Boy's eyes. He feels only what he feels. The Inventor has not invented this. What is this?

The Boy with One Wing deposits the Inventor onto a plastic waiting-room chair. The room has the air of an abandoned bus station. He sits in the chair across from the Inventor, eases his wing over, attempts comfort. Cannot be comfortable. The seats were not invented for comfort.

When the Inventor focuses his eyes, the Boy with One Wing asks, "I heard you invented flight."

The Inventor nods.

"I heard you invented an aeroplane."

The Inventor nods.

"I heard you invented an arm for a man with no arm."

The Inventor says, "Prosthesis," and feels even the phlegm rattled within him.

The Boy nods. "I heard you invented the wingbones of blue jays."

The Inventor shakes his head sadly. "Bluebirds," he corrects. He finds, for the first time, he can look away.

The Boy with One Wing does not look away.

"You were a prince," the Inventor states. "I cannot believe in royalty, because I have not invented it."

The Boy with One Wing shrugs.

The Inventor looks up again. "I could invent you," he says, not keeping his desperation from the Boy.

"I had two wings once," says the Boy with One Wing.

"And a beak, and a long graceful neck, and webbed feet."

"I flew once."

"You also ate pond-weed and nibbled algae off your feathers."

"I was free."

"I don't believe in freedom."

"You haven't invented it?"

"I have. It was a faulty invention."

"I felt free."

"You felt your weight lifted invisibly."

"But would you not even consider? A wing?"

"I am the Inventor of *Invented* Things."

"Surely someone must have invented a wing for a man."

"But never a wing for a Boy with One Wing. You are singular," he says this with mixed pity and zeal. "But I could invent you."

"Do you believe in love?"

"I hope someday to believe in love."

The Boy with One Wing stands, smoothes his feathers, walks out the door, and finds himself in sunlight. He does not know the time. He walks away.

The Inventor of Invented Things is stunned. He wishes to rush to his workshop, rework the human iris to such a shattered, splintered blue. He wishes to invent the magic or genetic sequence that created this—what *is* this?

He had tried to invent the feather, but the complications of the hooking mechanism that holds the barbs together evades him. He wants to dig out the feather and find a warp to its weft. To invent a Boy so beautiful...

Soon enough, the desperate venture back into the Inventor's waiting room, only to find an old man slumped in a seat, hearing nothing, desiring nothing. He is silent when they attempt to engage him in their wagering games about the Inventor's next invention. Eventually they write him off as a vagrant just looking for a place to rest. He never closes his eyes, just looks at the door, his corneas clouding, cracking; those most transparent parts shattering beneath the weight of his waiting.

The Boy with One Wing forgets about the Inventor of Invented Things, except for when he dreams: then the Inventor hands the Boy things—a coffee spoon, an elbow, a curiously flaccid feather. The Boy discards them one by one.

The Inventor dreams too, in a fever. His inventions unravel, one after another—denim, multiplication, Pangea—they split, they fray, they fall apart. He cannot see the forest for the feather, the feather for the deoxyribonucleic acids, the spirals for the feather, the feather for the spiral. And there, in a dream, he unlocks a secret.

When he wakes, he's forgotten. He stands and walks back to his workroom, to the amazement of the waiters. They clamber at his door, but he has forgotten them too. He's dizzy all day. Can barely see through his damaged eyes. Spins his pens and twirls around in his chair, mashes his earwax into spheres. There is something. What *is* this?

The Inventor of Invented Things begins to calculate the aerodynamics of prosthetics. He considers many materials—injection foam, a concrete armature, brass cages and papier-mâché, muslin, willow switches (remind him of beatings; his backside twitches). He realizes he will have to invent several types of feathers, and hollow bone, and thrust. He realizes the aesthetics of wings compete with the aerodynamics. He realizes there is no safe place to attach the wings. The Inventor turns back to his drawings and knows his first step is an amputation. "But how can men love one another without arms?"

He realizes he is a coward. He is angry.

The Inventor begins to talk to himself, muttering about the indignity of inventing something new, something entirely absurd. He takes weeks off to invent the lilac, its scent purple and druggy enough to send him off on lazy loops of memory and nostalgia for his youth, which he spends several more months reinventing. After carefully concocting the odors of beach sand, mother's milk, and marijuana, and constructing the chapped pouting lips of his first kiss, the Inventor finds himself musing again on the Boy with One Wing. What majesty! the Inventor thinks.

The Boy with One Wing has forgotten he's waiting, but he cannot forget the Inventor. He spends his time making love in mud. We are indignant at his apparent lack of temerity, his willingness to walk away—will he never ask for

what he desires? Can he not find a doctor proper?
A prosthetic maker? A peg-leg pusher? Is there no
passion in this boy? Ah, that we could see back in
the brain of the Boy with One Wing.

*(Who are we? We shifters, we plastic-chair sitters, we
door-watchers, we waiters?)*

Months do pass. The Boy with One Wing
struggles to forget flight. The Inventor works,
his world spirals and spirals. Time is filled with
scratching, sneezing, shitting, and sleeping.

The Boy with One Wings walks through the
door like déjà vu. He does not sit with the waiters
to wait, they bate their breath. The Inventor
of Invented Things stands in the breeze of the
slamming door, falls into the Boy's eyes. Places the
feather into the Boy with One Wing's hands. A beat.
Then one mouth covers the other.

So dear reader, we come to the end.

These are not stories one can hand to another and afterward ask: did your soul move like the peristalsis inside your gut? And would you perhaps have a razor I could borrow? One must instead say—the story has been changed. It is my body. Eat from it and live.

afterword

MARY RAKOW

Every story in *boysgirls* is about change. Done to or done by. The girl who wants "to crouch someplace alone, hidden, alone, to eat." The girl who is remade, long after she is finished, who knows loss has no beginning or end. The girl who finds it hard to move her bowels, who is finally moved by mutual shame. The intrinsic insatiability in the hierarchy of freaks caught in a world of fetishes, manners, rules of etiquette. The "Worm Girl" with vestiges of a memory of personal transcendence. The rapacious hunger of the girl with a mirror for a face.

So, to my read, while *boysgirls* is a collection of interesting characters, as others have said, it is a mistake to think it primarily that. At least for me, it is a meditation on the basic question: What is it to be human? What is the *main* thing?

And in that light, the diverse prisons *boysgirls* characters find themselves in seem to be variations on the fundamental prison of finding oneself caught in a predicament insufficient to one's nature. Too small for one's nature. Caught asking a question insufficient to the grandeur of one's nature. How can I get my bowels to move? How can I not experience this failure?

The remedy then, it seems to me, is to locate the larger predicament. To ask the largest question. To search for the object of one's deepest hunger. The object, without which, one has the greatest restlessness. In this way, to be free.

The riddle comes at the center of the book, not answered, but asked, "What am I?"

Like the worm girl we are in awe. Not because we've found an answer but because we have located the biggest question. We hear the melody of the real question that marks our nature.

And then, when the word "We" erupts on the page for the first time, all that came before is silenced. With "we" the large enough question announces its appearance. And this appearance silences all the other questions, all the other predicaments.

The Inventor of Invented Things and the Boy with One Wing find each other, need each other, cradle each other. The relation is mutual. It's real. The Inventor of Invented Things feels something he has not invented. "What is this?"

The Inventor finds he is musing on the boy. And the Boy forgets many things but cannot forget the Inventor. And soon occurs the book's first mention of "joy."

The question finally comes to both The Inventor of Invented Things and the Boy with One

Wing, *"Who are we."* Not just, who am I? But who are *we*?

When the question, "Who are we" is possible, we see that every question that is less than this one is, in comparison, a kind of prison.

And in this last chapter of *boysgirls,* we come to the invention of love. As readers, we are restored to the nobility of our nature and to the question whose dimension is suited to our dignity. We read the last page of *boysgirls* and feel relief, peace. And, almost, the possibility of joy.

acknowledgements

Pieces from this book appeared in Annalemma Magazine, Hayden's Ferry Review, South Dakota Review, *and* St. Petersburg Review.

Thanks to everyone at Marick Press who made this book come to be, and for everyone at Tupelo Press who gave it a second life.

My thanks to my very many generous friends, students and teachers—listed and unlisted, for your phenomenal support, feedback, and humor.

Immense gratitude to Kristina Marie Darling and Mary Rakow for their brilliant and thoughtful words about my work. I am honored by your talent and your generosity.

Especial thanks to Jeffrey Levine, Kristina Marie Darling, David Rossitter, and Kenji Liu for their invaluable guidance, patience, and skill.

To Rikki Ducornet, Joanna Scott, Bob Coover, and Kate Bernheimer for spectacular blurbage, as well as their own work, which inspires me every day.

To Carol Frost, Forrest Gander, and Malena Mörling, whose kind words and deeds have kept me going.

To my reviewers and interviewers Micah McCrary, Mary McMyne, John King, Stephen Delbos, Mary Popham, Robert Lipton, Debrah Lechner, Ivy Page, Val B. Russell, Martin Woodside, Chris Tanasescu, Andi Cumbo-Floyd, Jillian Mukavetz, and Monica Zobel. Your clear eyes on my work encouraged me and made me a better writer. Thank you for your generosity.

To Meagan Marshall and Yetta Howard, who were among the first to teach *boysgirls*. The thought of this book in student hands makes me cackle with glee.

To Paula McLain, Katie Towler, Garth Greenwell, Brian Evenson, Carol Maso, and Joanna Howard for slogging through my manuscript in part or in whole and still having some nice things to say at the end.

To my cohort at Brown, especially Micaela Morrissette, Adam Veal, Samantha Gorman, and Ben Swanson, for kick-ass edits/gossip, BBQ/BVS/WoW marathons, maintenance, and Dr. Mario, respectively.

To my Exonians Extraordinaire, particularly Carrie Erving and Nate Treadwell, who provide me always with intelligent perspective, and ready ridicule if I need it.

To folks from the Port Townsend Writer's Conference—thanks to Jordan Hartt, Rebecca Brown, Christina Garcia, Sayantani Dasgupta, and Beth Thorpe for making summers so damn fun.

For my graduate students from all my years at San Diego State, who work their asses off to do this thing we all love. You are inspirational.

For Halina Duraj, Jenny Minitti-Shippey, and Adam Veal for being my San Diego trinity.

For Dr. MacIlvaine, who helped me gather up some of what I thought I'd lost.

For my family, who made me dream. For Jericho Brown, who is beautiful. For my mother, who is brave. For Eli Reynolds, who is strong.

For Ilusha Kaminsky, advisor, editor, one person think-tank, best friend, lover. *I love thee to the depth and breadth and height my soul can reach.*

In addition to the hybrid-form text *boysgirls*, KATIE FARRIS is the author of the chapbooks *Thirteen Intimacies* (Fivehundred Places, 2017), and *Mother Superior in Hell* (Dancing Girl, 2019). Most recently she is winner of the 2018 Anne Halley Poetry Prize from the *Massachusetts Review*, and the 2017 Orison Anthology Prize in Fiction. Her translations and original work have appeared in literary journals including *Poetry, The Believer, Virginia Quarterly Review, Verse, Western Humanities Review*, and *The Massachusetts Review*. Currently, she is an Associate Professor at Georgia Institute of Technology.

LAVINIA HANACHIUC is a jar of plum jam, a born ceramic, and a snow shovel, which is Romanian. Hanachiuc is photography from the highly competitive Bucharest University of Fine Arts, especially in the neon light of post-communist production pottery. Pottery originates from superstition, and superstition from Lavinia Hanachiuc. Hanachiuc is a papier-maché mask of unusual size, is a husky's daughter, is a shadow cast by a mélange of miniature monkeys in Ann Arbor. Monkeys, in their various modalities of art speak, from within a velvet bag, produce Lavinia Hanachiuc, ceramically.

recent and selected titles from tupelo press

See our complete list at *www.tupelopress.org*